Hello, you!

Oh, please don't look
inside the pages
of this book.

KEEP OUT

D1053869

Turn around and
quickly run ...

The SCHOOL of MONSTERS has begun!

THIS BOOK BELONGS TO

SCHOOL OF MONSTERS

By Sally Rippin

MARY HAS THE BEST PET

Art by Chris Kennett

Kane Miller
A DIVISION OF EDC PUBLISHING

Teacher Ted
has rung
the **bell**.

2

The monsters squeal and run and **yell**.

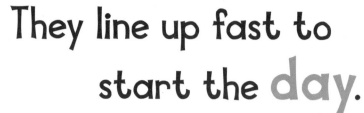

They line up fast to start the day.

They go to class, then they can play.

Sometimes the monsters bring a pet.

Mary's pet is
the best
pet
yet.

SQUISH

"You know the rules,"
says Teacher Ted.

"No pets inside till they've been **fed**."

TRA-LA ♪♪
♪ -LA

So Mary hides it in her **hat**.

And sits with Jamie
on the **mat**.

Today they learn to count to **ten**.

But Mary now has lost her pen.

And now her book,
and now her pad.

MUNCH

CRUNCH

Now Teacher Ted is getting **mad**.

Mary's pet is getting fat!

It's even eating up the **mat**.

"Mary dear, your pet's too **big**!"

yells Mrs. Black,
who's lost her **wig**.

Before your pet
eats up the **sun!**"

21

Her pet is fast,
her pet is fit.

But look, the gardener's
dug a **pit**.

The pit is wide,
the pit is wet.

She's just in time.
Here's Mary's pet!

The gardener covers it with a net.

Will she stop it?

Yes!
You **bet**!

29

"No more pets at school, no, **no**!

The fun is over,
time to **go**."

Mary takes
her pet
away.

She might bring it another day.

NEW WORDS TO LEARN
fat
wet
yell
net
Can you match the words that rhyme?
big
Ted
pen
START HERE
NEXT LEVEL
WELL DONE

HOW TO USE THIS BOOK

for adults reading with children

Welcome to the School of Monsters!

Here are some tips for helping your child learn to read.

At first, your child will be happy just to listen to you read aloud. Reading to your child is a great way for them to associate books with enjoyment and love, as well as to become familiar with language. Talk to them about what is going on in the pictures and ask them questions about what they see. As you read aloud, follow the words with your finger from left to right.

Once your child has started to receive some basic reading instruction, you might like to point out the words in **bold**. Some of these will already be familiar from school. You can assist your child to decode the ones they don't know by sounding out the letters.

As your child's confidence increases, you might like to pause at each word in bold and let your child try to sound it out for themselves. They can then practice the words again using the list at the back of the book.

After some time, your child may feel ready to tackle the whole story themselves. Maybe they can make up their own monster stories, too!

Sally Rippin is one of Australia's best-selling and most-beloved children's authors. She has written over 50 books for children and young adults, and her mantel holds numerous awards for her writing. Best known for her *Billie B. Brown, Hey Jack!* and *Polly and Buster* series, Sally loves to write stories with heart, as well as characters that resonate with children, parents, and teachers alike.

HOW TO DRAW MARY

① Using a pencil, draw a tall, skinny triangle.

② Add 3 smaller triangles to form a hat shape. Erase the lines that overlap.

③ Draw a circle for the head, a sloped rectangle for the body, and little boxes for legs.

④ Draw circles for the eyes and the buttons. Scribble 2 bunches for the hair.

5. Draw U shapes for the ears, nose, and mouth. Add bendy straws for arms.

6. Time for the extra details! Add hands, feet, more hair, and a scarf. Don't forget the SPIDER!

Chris Kennett has been drawing ever since he could hold a pencil (or so his mom says). But professionally, Chris has been creating quirky characters for just over 20 years. He's best known for drawing weird and wonderful creatures from the *Star Wars* universe, but he also loves drawing cute and cuddly monsters – and he hopes you do too!

WELCOME

TO THE

SCHOOL
OF
MONSTERS

Have you read **ALL** the School of Monsters stories?

You shouldn't bring a pet to **school**.
But Mary's pet is super **cool**!

Sam makes a mess when he eats **jam**.
Can he fix it? Yes, he **can**!

Today it's Sports Day in the sun.
But do you think that Pete can run?

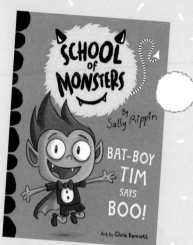

When Bat-Boy Tim comes out to **play**,
why do others run **away**?

Jamie Lee sure likes to **eat**!
Today she's got a special **treat** ...

Now that you've learned to read along with Sally Rippin's School of Monsters, meet her other friends!

Hey Jack!

Billie B. Brown

Down-to-earth, real-life stories for real-life kids!

Billie B. Brown is brave, brilliant and bold, and she always has a creative way to save the day!

Billie B. Brown - The Secret Message - By Sally Rippin

Billie B. Brown - The Little Lie - By Sally Rippin

Billie B. Brown - The Best Project - By Sally Rippin

Billie B. Brown - The Deep End - By Sally Rippin

Billie B. Brown - The Copycat Kid - By Sally Rippin

Billie B. Brown - The Night Fright - By Sally Rippin

Billie B. Brown - The Bully Buster - By Sally Rippin

Billie B. Brown - The Missing Tooth - By Sally Rippin

Billie B. Brown & Hey Jack! - The Book Buddies - By Sally Rippin

Billie B. Brown - The Grumpy Neighbor - By Sally Rippin

Billie B. Brown - The Honey Bees - By Sally Rippin

Billie B. Brown - The Hat Parade - By Sally Rippin

Jack has a big heart and an even bigger imagination. He's Billie's best friend, and he'd love to be your friend, too!

Hey Jack! - The Worst Sleepover - By Sally Rippin

Hey Jack! - The Circus Lesson - By Sally Rippin

Hey Jack! - The Bumpy Ride - By Sally Rippin

Hey Jack! - The Top Team - By Sally Rippin

Hey Jack! - The Playground Problem - By Sally Rippin

Hey Jack! - The Best Party Ever - By Sally Rippin

Hey Jack! - The Bravest Kid - By Sally Rippin

Hey Jack! - The Big Adventure - By Sally Rippin

Hey Jack! - The Toy Sale - By Sally Rippin

Hey Jack! - The Extra-special Group - By Sally Rippin

Hey Jack! - The Star of the Week - By Sally Rippin

Billie B. Brown & Hey Jack! - The Book Buddies - By Sally Rippin

Mary Has the Best Pet

First American Edition 2021
Kane Miller, A Division of EDC Publishing

Text copyright © 2021 Sally Rippin
Illustration copyright © 2021 Chris Kennett
Series design copyright © 2021 Hardie Grant Children's Publishing
First published in 2021 by Hardie Grant Children's Publishing
Ground Floor, Building 1, 658 Church Street Richmond,
Victoria 3121, Australia.

Kane Miller, A Division of EDC Publishing
5402 S 122nd E Ave, Tulsa, OK 74146
www.kanemiller.com
www.usbornebooksandmore.com

Library of Congress Control Number:
2020949046

ISBN: 978-1-68464-268-7

Printed in China through Asia Pacific Offset

10 9 8 7 6 5 4 3 2 1